P9-AQB-853

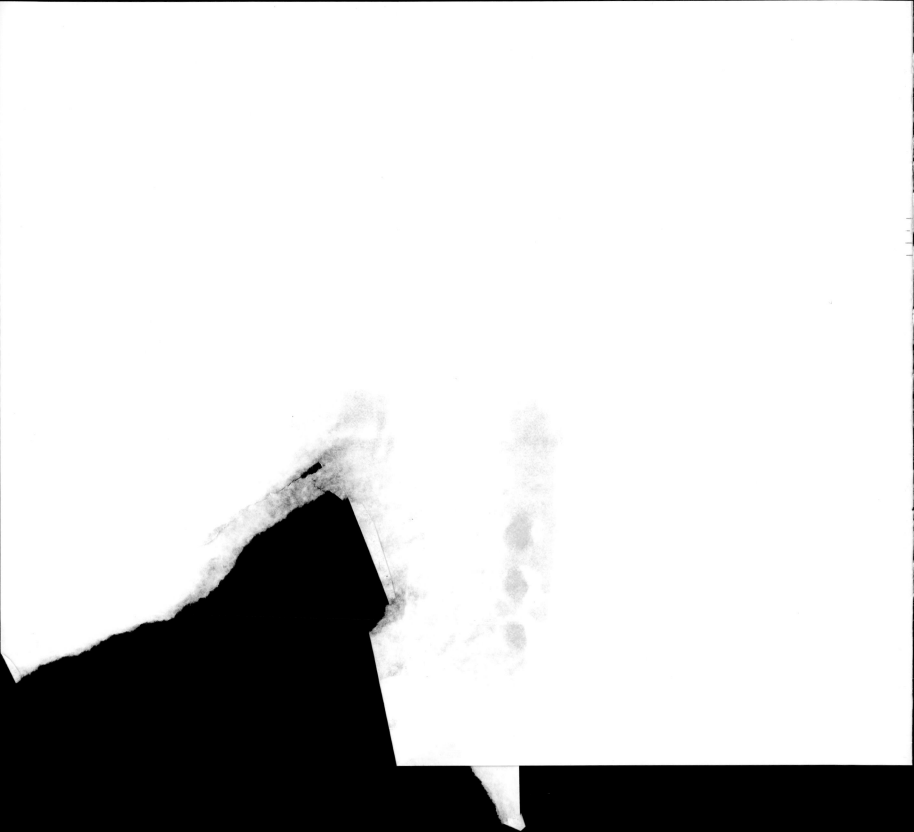

A FIDDLE FOR ANGUS

BUDGE WILSON

ART BY SUSAN TOOKE

TUNDRA BOOKS

Published in Canada by Tundra Books,
481 University Avenue, Toronto, Ontario M5G 2E9

Published in the United States by Tundra Books of Northern New York,
P.O. Box 1030, Plattsburgh, New York 12901

Library of Congress Card Number: 2001086823

National Library of Canada Cataloguing in Publication Data

Wilson, Budge
   A fiddle for Angus

ISBN 0-88776-500-9

I. Tooke, Susan. II. Title.

PS8595.I5813F52 2001   jC813'.54   C2001-930075-1
PZ7.W54Fi 2001

We acknowledge the support of the Canada Council for the Arts and
the Ontario Arts Council for our publishing program.

We acknowledge the financial support of the Government of Canada through the
Book Publishing Industry Development Program for our publishing activities.

"Song For The Mira": Words and music by Allister MacGillivray,
published by Cabot Trail Music, administered by Morning Music Limited.

Design: Terri-Anne Fong

Medium: acrylic on watercolor paper

Printed and bound in Hong Kong

1 2 3 4 5 6   06 05 04 03 02 01

For Norene Smiley,
great guru
of Atlantic children's writers.
B.W.

For my father, George Tooke,
who gave me his love,
my Canadian heritage,
and my grandfather's fiddle.
S.T.

———————————————

Susan Tooke would like to thank
the fiddlers of Cape Breton and the
musical community of Nova Scotia for their help,
patience, and inspiration.

Tooke

Angus lived in a Cape Breton village, right beside the sea. All around him there were boats and water and high hills.

Angus's family was musical. Mom played the accordion. Dad played the whistle. Molly sang songs in a high clear voice, which was beautiful enough to make you cry. Tom played the guitar.

Angus was way smaller than they were. He listened. Sometimes he hummed. Humming was fun. He loved all the music that his family was making.

But after a while, Angus started to feel a little bit sad. His family orchestra was wonderful, but he wasn't really in it. He knew all the tunes by heart, but suddenly humming just wasn't good enough. He didn't love humming anymore.

Angus started looking angry when his family was playing and Molly was singing. He crossed his arms and pretended not to listen. He looked at them all with his brows screwed together. He refused to hum. "I don't like this music anymore," he thought.

Finally, the family noticed that the humming had stopped. Mom squeezed her accordion shut and said, "Why aren't you humming, Angus? We need your beautiful hum. We miss it." She held him close to her, and smiled.

Angus sighed. He didn't hug her back. "It's not enough," he said. "It's not special."

Molly stopped singing and said, "It *is so*. It's very special. It's just as important as singing."

Tom hunkered down beside Angus and said, "We love your humming. We need it. It's one of our instruments."

The next evening, the family played for a while on the
wharf. Angus was crouched down on an orange buoy,
feeling miserable.

His dad came across to him, and leaned over. "We've decided
something. Something you'll like," said Dad. "Guess what?"

Angus sat right up, and his eyes were wide-open and
bright. *"What?"* He almost yelled it.

Dad grinned. So did Mom and Molly and Tom. "We're going
to get you an instrument. It'll be your very own. You're big
enough now. You can choose."

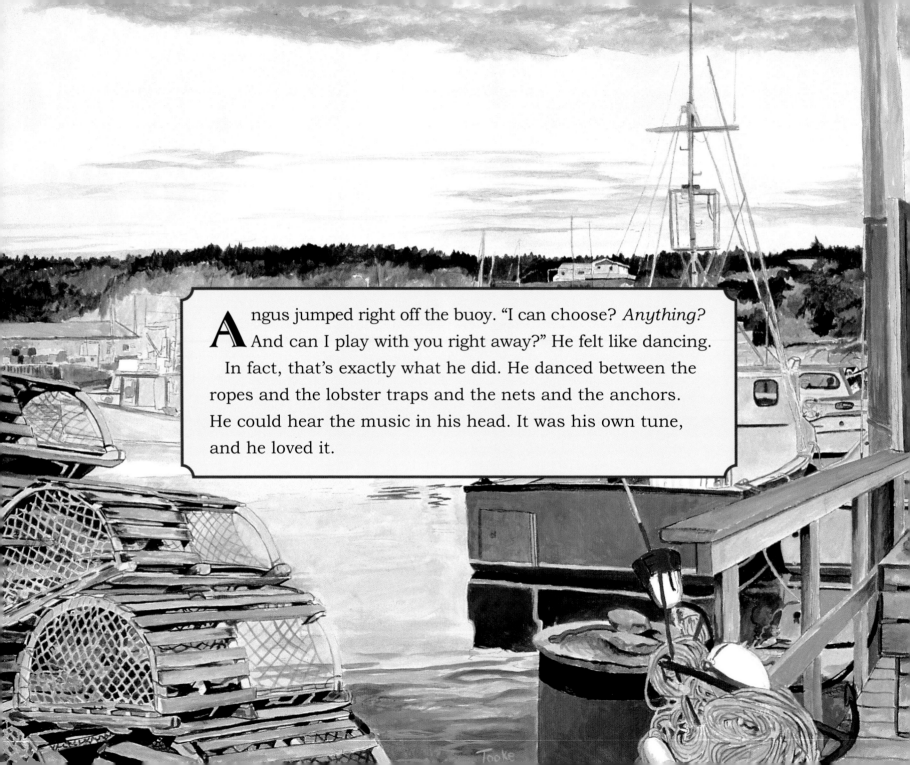

Angus jumped right off the buoy. "I can choose? *Anything?* And can I play with you right away?" He felt like dancing. In fact, that's exactly what he did. He danced between the ropes and the lobster traps and the nets and the anchors. He could hear the music in his head. It was his own tune, and he loved it.

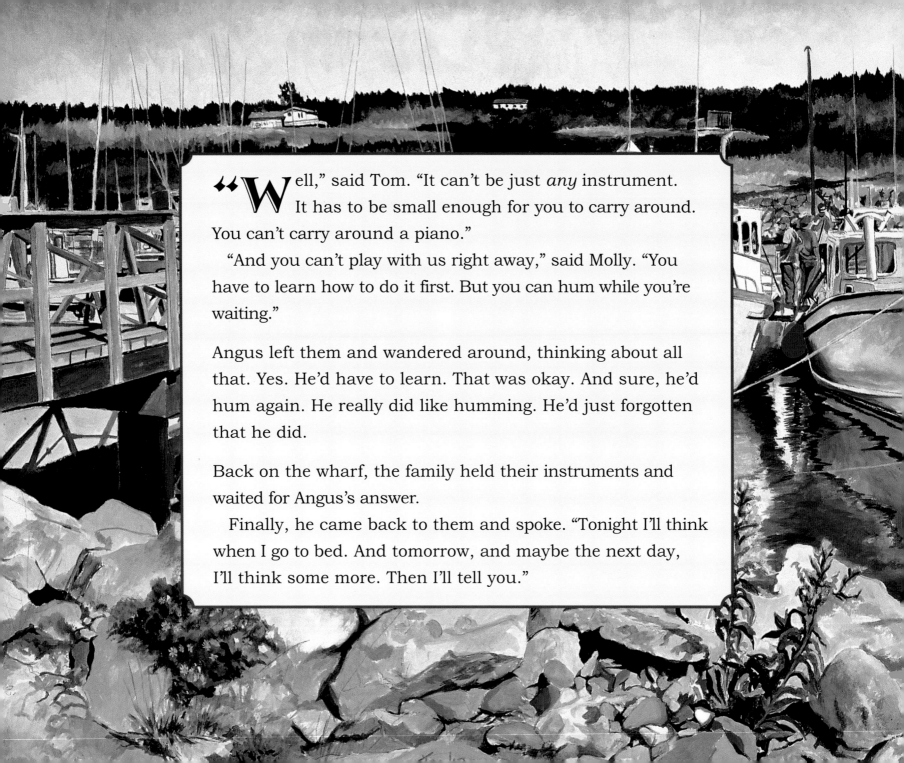

"Well," said Tom. "It can't be just *any* instrument. It has to be small enough for you to carry around. You can't carry around a piano."

"And you can't play with us right away," said Molly. "You have to learn how to do it first. But you can hum while you're waiting."

Angus left them and wandered around, thinking about all that. Yes. He'd have to learn. That was okay. And sure, he'd hum again. He really did like humming. He'd just forgotten that he did.

Back on the wharf, the family held their instruments and waited for Angus's answer.

Finally, he came back to them and spoke. "Tonight I'll think when I go to bed. And tomorrow, and maybe the next day, I'll think some more. Then I'll tell you."

The following morning, Angus went down to the beach because that was his favorite place. He needed to think about his instrument.

Angus looked up and down. He listened. The waves churned and swished back into themselves, and then pounded forward on the sand. The sandpipers made their own sounds as they skittered across the beach. The seagulls called and squawked and moaned and chattered. The wind sighed among the evergreens, and whispered as it moved through the beach grasses. The big red groaner buoy sang a deep and sorrowful song.

He listened to all those sounds, and he loved them all. But they didn't tell him which instrument to choose.

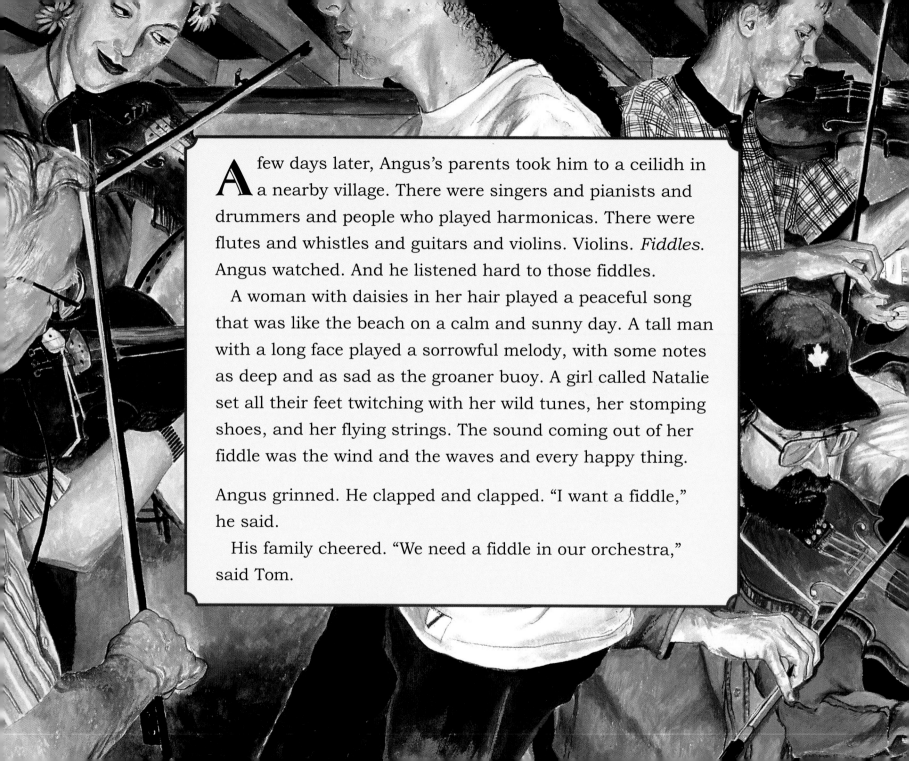

A few days later, Angus's parents took him to a ceilidh in a nearby village. There were singers and pianists and drummers and people who played harmonicas. There were flutes and whistles and guitars and violins. Violins. *Fiddles.* Angus watched. And he listened hard to those fiddles.

A woman with daisies in her hair played a peaceful song that was like the beach on a calm and sunny day. A tall man with a long face played a sorrowful melody, with some notes as deep and as sad as the groaner buoy. A girl called Natalie set all their feet twitching with her wild tunes, her stomping shoes, and her flying strings. The sound coming out of her fiddle was the wind and the waves and every happy thing.

Angus grinned. He clapped and clapped. "I want a fiddle," he said.

His family cheered. "We need a fiddle in our orchestra," said Tom.

So Angus got his fiddle. He got it right away, even though it wasn't his birthday. Everyone stood around smiling when it was handed to him.

Angus picked up his fiddle and tucked it under his chin, like he'd seen Big Murdoch MacDougall do. Big Murdoch MacDougall lived in a house beside the Government Wharf.

"It's all tuned and ready," said Dad. "But it isn't easy. You'll need lessons."

Angus paid no attention. He shut his eyes and lifted the bow. He was going to make the most beautiful music in the world.

Then Angus drew the bow across the strings. *Squawk! Screech! Eeeeek!* Angus was so surprised that he almost dropped the bow. The fiddle sounded like a gull whose fish had been stolen. It was like the harsh cry of a heron.

"Where is the music hiding?" asked Angus, with tears in his eyes.

"It's inside," said Dad.

"It just has to be coaxed out," said Molly.

"It takes a while to learn how to do it," said Tom.

"But if you want it really hard, and if you work for it, it'll come out for you. You'll see," said Mom.

"I want it," said Angus. "I'll work."

So Angus took fiddle lessons. He took them from Big Murdoch MacDougall, who didn't use sheet music, or books with notes written down. He just knew how to do it.

Angus wanted really hard. He worked hard. He got better. He sat on a rock on the beach, or on the bed in his room, or stood in front of the window. He practiced hour after hour. Day after day. Week after week.

When the family orchestra played in the evenings, Angus held the fiddle in his lap, just so it would know he loved it, even if the music wasn't quite ready to come out of it yet. In the meantime, he did a lot of humming.

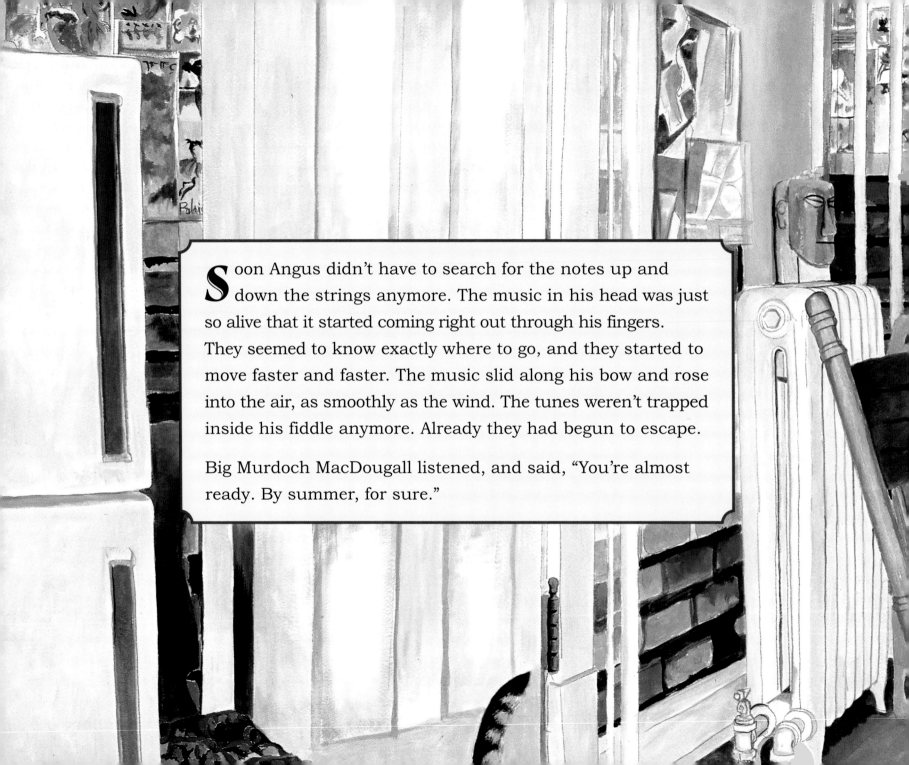

Soon Angus didn't have to search for the notes up and down the strings anymore. The music in his head was just so alive that it started coming right out through his fingers. They seemed to know exactly where to go, and they started to move faster and faster. The music slid along his bow and rose into the air, as smoothly as the wind. The tunes weren't trapped inside his fiddle anymore. Already they had begun to escape.

Big Murdoch MacDougall listened, and said, "You're almost ready. By summer, for sure."

One evening in June, Angus went down to the beach, where his family was playing a song he knew and loved. He stood in front of them, holding the fiddle under his chin. They stopped playing and Molly stopped singing. "Well?" they said.

"I'm ready," said Angus. He started to play. It was a wild jig, but his fingers had learned to race up and down the strings like ripples over the water.

"Let's do 'Song For The Mira,'" said Angus. This was a sad song with a happy ending. "Just like me," thought Angus, as Molly sang the last verse. "I'm a happy end to a sad story."

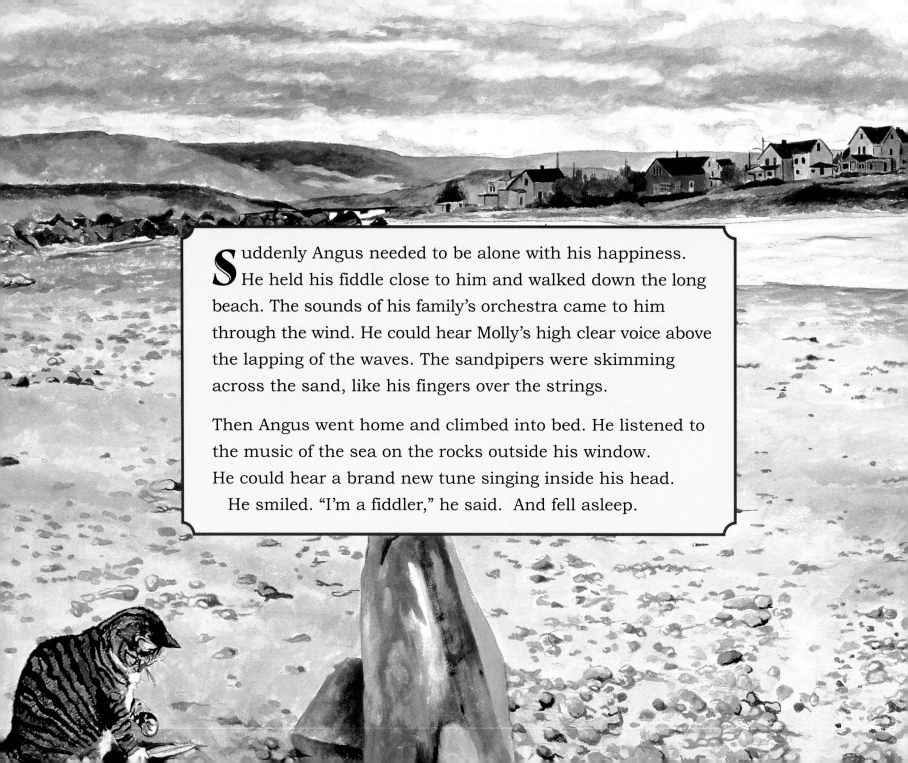

Suddenly Angus needed to be alone with his happiness. He held his fiddle close to him and walked down the long beach. The sounds of his family's orchestra came to him through the wind. He could hear Molly's high clear voice above the lapping of the waves. The sandpipers were skimming across the sand, like his fingers over the strings.

Then Angus went home and climbed into bed. He listened to the music of the sea on the rocks outside his window. He could hear a brand new tune singing inside his head.

He smiled. "I'm a fiddler," he said. And fell asleep.